The Soul Thieves

Roger Hurn

Illustrated by Kenny Kiernan

Ransm

Kelly Montez

Like · Comment · Friend

Hey, I'm Kelly Montez, and unless you've been living in a cave for the past year you'll know I'm in the band *GirlFriendZ*.

Yeah, that's right, I'm the one with the killer looks and a voice like gravel dipped in honey. And *GirlFriendZ* is the number one band in the world – or it *was*, until the day the aliens invaded Earth and banned music! Those creepoids are *so* not cool.

But don't worry guys, we're not going to let them get away with that. *GirlFriendZ* will carry on making music and there's no way a bunch of alien weirdos in MIB (Music is Banned) is going to stop us!

M

GirlFriendZ
The Soul Thieves
by Roger Hurn
Illustrated by Kenny Kiernan

Published by Ransom Publishing Ltd.
Radley House, 8 St. Cross Road, Winchester, Hampshire
SO23 9HX, UK
www.ransom.co.uk

ISBN   978 178127 151 3
First published in 2013

Yaz Jackson

Like · Comment · Friend

Hiya guys, Yaz here. I was born in a circus and my mum and dad were acrobats, so that's why I'm always doing somersaults, cartwheels and back flips on stage. On our next tour I'm gonna walk across the stage on a high wire! How cool is that?

Yeah, you did hear me right. There WILL be another *GirlFriendZ* tour – just as soon as we find a way to send the Zargons back to their home planet with their creepy alien tails between their legs.

Olivia Parsons

Like · Comment · Friend

Hi *GirlFriendZ* fans. My name is Olivia – but everyone calls me Liv. I know I look like the girl next door, but I can be a bit of a wild child when it comes to music! I just love getting up on stage and singing my heart out!

But now those freaky aliens are arresting musicians and destroying all the musical instruments they can get their tentacles on! It makes me so mad, but they'll never catch us and stop us singing.

That's a promise!

Eve Rossi

Like · Comment · Friend

Hello everybody. I'm Eve, the girl with the crazy hair and the personality to match!

It's great being in *GirlFriendZ* 'cos it gives me the chance to wear all kinds of amazing outfits. I love designing my own clothes and it gives me a buzz when I see you guys copying my look!

I know the Zargons are trying to stop us having fun – but don't fret guys, we are *so* gonna have the last laugh!

Charlotte Opirah

Like · Comment · Friend

OK, it's me, Charlotte. Usually I'd rather sing than talk, 'cos I'm the best singer in the band. Hey, just kidding!!

But I've got something to say that can't be put into a song. It's this. We absolutely *have* to find a way to beat the Zargons! They must have a weakness – and I've got a suspicion it has something to do with music.

Think about it guys. They have banned music and they're doing some kind of alien mind-wipe, so musicians and singers forget how to play and sing. Why? Well, I'm gonna make it my business to find out!

8

Finn the roadie

Like · Comment · Friend

Hey, I'm Finn and I have the best job in the world. I'm the *roadie* (that's road manager) for *GirlFriendZ*. Well, it *was* the best job until the Zargons arrived and we had to go on the run. Now my job is about getting the girls to their secret gigs *and* keeping them out of the Zargon's clutches! You see, the Zargon agents of MIB track down musicians and singers and take them off to the 'harmony' camps to have their minds wiped. Then, when they come out of the camps, they can't remember how to play or sing.

GirlFriendZ are the last band left, so MIB are desperate to catch them. If they do that, then that really *will* be the day music dies. But I'm never going to let that happen!

The Zargons

The Zargons are an alien race from the Andromeda galaxy. They have developed advanced technology that enables their starships to travel faster than the speed of light.

They are humanoid in appearance and, contrary to popular opinion, they do not possess tentacles (or tails!). However, in certain conditions, their eyes glow like cats' eyes.

They are on a mission to eradicate all forms of music from the universe. To this end, the Zargons build 'harmony' camps on the planets they invade. Anyone with musical talent is taken to the camps by Zargon agents of MIB (*Music Is Banned*), where they are subjected to a process known as 'mind wiping'. The mind–wipe has the effect of making the musician or singer forget how to play or sing. In street slang this process is known as 'soul stealing'.

The main feature of the 'harmony' camps are the giant incinerators where musical instruments are destroyed.

It is believed that the Zargons' hatred of music stems from the fact that music is the only thing that has the power to defeat them. (See article: *vampires*, *garlic*, *crosses*.)

Prologue

London, England. Saturday 2nd August 2025

'Thank you Wembley. It's been emotional.'

Kelly punched the air with her fist and 70,000 fans screamed back at her. Yaz, Olivia, Eve and Charlotte, the other members of *GirlFriendZ*, jumped up and down on the stage like hyperactive kangaroos. Waves of love washed over them from their fans. If they hadn't known they were the world's biggest band before this gig – they knew it now!

'Hey, listen to those guys,' yelled Charlotte.

'Yay, it's awesome,' Eve yelled back at her.

Olivia grinned like a cat with a bowl of double cream. 'It just doesn't get any better than this.'

'Yes it does,' said Yaz. 'This show's being beamed worldwide by satellite. Billions of people are going mad for us.'

* * * * * * *

Suddenly a huge shadow covered the stadium. The howling crowd fell silent. A giant starship hovered over Wembley.

At first people thought it was part of the show. But then a red laser light shot out from the ship and vapourised the Wembley

arch. A metallic voice rang out into the
stunned silence.

'People of Earth, go to your homes and
stay there. This is an order. Failure to obey
will be punishable by death. This planet is
now a province of the Zargon Empire.'

One

The Gig

You don't expect to turn the corner of a back street in a run-down part of the city and find *GirlFriendZ*, the most famous band in the world, playing a gig. But that's exactly what happened to the lucky shoppers who'd come to buy their fruit and vegetables at Tudorgate market.

Kelly, Eve, Yaz, Charlotte and Liv were standing on a stage made of wooden boxes, belting out a string of their hits to a delighted crowd.

While the people danced and clapped along with the girls, Finn, their road manager, stood at the side of the makeshift stage watching anxiously for trouble. He wasn't worried about the audience; he was worried about agents from MIB. MIB was the organisation set up by the Zargon invaders to crush music – and they were desperate to catch the girls and mind-wipe them.

GirlFriendZ had been hiding out in a small flat in a tower block in the east end of the city. But they'd been going stir crazy cooped up in such a small place. After all, until recently the girls had only stayed at luxury five-star hotels. It was while they were there that Charlotte had had her 'brilliant' idea.

'Hey, guys, let's do a gig in the market. Only humans go there. The Zargons are such a bunch of freaks I bet they don't even eat fruit and veg.'

'Good thinking, Char!' enthused Kelly. 'We can do a few numbers, give the local folks a treat and then be safely back here before the Zargons even know it.'

Finn had tried to veto the notion, but all the girls were too excited to listen to him. Now here they were doing what they loved best – singing their hearts out.

Suddenly the crowd whooped extra loudly. Yaz was performing her trade mark triple back somersault move. Finn was watching the stage and so he didn't see the MIB snatch squad sneaking through the crowd towards the girls!

Two

No Rights

Unlike the rest of the crowd, the Zargon snatch squad had thick lumps of wax stuffed in their ears. Music had the same effect on them that garlic and crosses had on vampires. But because the wax blocked out all sound, the MIB agents were safe.

They leapt up on stage and grabbed the girls and gagged them. The crowd stopped dancing and fell silent. They stared sullenly at the MIB squad. Then a young guy shouted out. 'Let the girls go, you Zargon losers. We want to hear them.'

The MIB captain removed the wax from his ears and pointed his long bony finger at him. 'Be quiet, human,' he growled. 'Or you will join these rebels in the 'harmony' camps.'

Everybody gasped. People looked at each other in horror.

'You can't mind-wipe *GirlFriendZ*,' shouted a woman angrily. 'Their music is the best. We have a right to listen to it.'

'You humans have no rights anymore,' snarled the captain. 'And, when we have finished with these girls, you will have no more music either!'

He pulled a strange device from his belt and a bolt of electricity sizzled over the heads of the crowd. People ran away in terror. They had no wish to be vapourised. But Finn didn't run. He picked up a rotten tomato from the ground and hurled it at the nearest MIB agent. It splattered all over the Zargon's face.

The agent let go of his grip on Yaz to wipe the mush from his eyes. This was a mistake on his part. Quicker than greased lightning, Yaz back flipped off the stage.

Finn grabbed her hand. 'Come on Yaz,' he yelled. 'Run!'

Three

The Camp

Yaz was bouncing up and down on her seat as Finn pushed his old bone-shaker of a van to its limit as they drove along the motorway.

Up ahead of them was a sleek black MIB cruiser. It was taking the other members of *GirlFriendZ* to a 'harmony' camp to have their minds wiped.

Finn made sure he kept several vehicles between the van and the alien wagon. He did not want the MIB agents to spot them.

The cruiser turned off the motorway and headed for the camp. Finn and Yaz followed it. The camp's tall incineration tower could be seen for miles. Smoke belched from it. Yaz knew that meant thousands of precious musical instruments were being destroyed.

'We can always make more musical instruments,' she thought. *'But once the Zargons have done their cruel soul-stealing trick on the girls, then they'll never sing again.'*

The cruiser arrived at the gates. They swung open and the cruiser drove inside. The gates shut behind it. Zargon guards patrolled the high perimeter fence while other MIB agents looked out of the watch-towers.

Finn and Yaz drove on past the entrance. They carried on along the road until they came to a bumpy track leading to a wood. Finn parked the van and slumped down in his seat. 'Sorry, Yaz,' he said. 'But it's hopeless. There's no way to get inside that place.'

But Yaz wasn't so sure. 'Oh, I think there is,' she said. 'But we'll have to wait for darkness for me to put my plan into operation.'

Four

The Plan

It was close to midnight when Yaz and Finn crept up to a big tree that stood next to the camp's perimeter fence.

'OK, we're here,' Finn whispered. 'But I still don't see how we're going to get inside the camp.'

'*We're* not,' replied Yaz. 'But *I* am.'

Finn frowned. 'How are you going to do that?'

Yaz grinned. 'Hey, you're forgetting that before I joined *GirlFriendZ*, I was a circus acrobat. First up, I'm going to climb this tree. Then I'm going step on to the top of the fence and walk along it like it was a high wire. Easy!'

Finn did not look convinced. 'OK,' he said. 'But even if you do get inside the camp you've got to knock out the guards and rescue the girls.'

Yaz held up a music data chip. 'Don't worry, Finn. I'm going to use this.'

Finn looked baffled. 'And just how is that going to help?'

Yaz pulled at her earlobe. 'Well, the Zargons want to steal our souls with their mind-wiping, so I'm going to use the

camp's loudspeaker system to give them a blast of soul music, *GirlFriendZ*-style! It's going to have the same effect on the Zargons as an anteater in a termite's nest.'

Finn nodded. 'Well, let's hope so. But while you're playing solo what am I supposed to do? Finn bit his knuckles with worry. 'And how are you going to get the girls out? They're not acrobats, so they can't climb the fence like you.'

Yaz reached out and punched him gently on his arm. 'Hey, don't stress. I've got it all figured out. When you hear it kicking off inside the camp I want you to ram the gates with the van and smash them open. We'll be there waiting for you.'

She looked anxiously at Finn. 'You're the getaway driver. So please don't mess up!'

Five

Soul Music

Finn turned and ran off to get the van while Yaz scrambled like a squirrel up the tree. In no time at all she had skipped along an outstretched branch and dropped lightly onto the top of the fence.

A sudden gust of wind caught her and she swayed wildly. For a second it seemed as if she would tumble and fall, but she regained her balance and, with her arms

held out from her sides, she carefully made
her way to the nearest watchtower.

The Zargon guard spun round as she
stepped inside, but before he could do
anything Yaz opened her mouth and sang a

perfect high 'C'. It was the note opera singers use to shatter glass.

The guard clapped his hands over his ears and Yaz popped the data chip into the loudspeaker console. She flipped the switch and *GirlFriendZ'* sweet soul music blasted out at top volume from every speaker in the camp.

Immediately, the Zargons came stumbling out into the open, desperately seeking the source of their torment. But the music was driving them mad. They crashed into each other and became more and more helpless. Some of them even began to dissolve into a jelly-like sludge.

Yaz shinned down the steps of the watchtower and raced to the detention block. None of the MIB agents tried to stop her; they were all too busy trying to save themselves.

Yaz ran down a long corridor until she came to a series of cells. She used a key from one of the unconscious guards to deactivate the locks. The doors slid open and Eve, Liv, Charlotte and Kelly stepped

out, along with all the other musicians and singers the Zargons had imprisoned.

'Hey, guys, it's mass breakout time!' yelled Yaz.

Nobody said a word of thanks. They all were wearing gags. The MIB guards couldn't risk them singing. But it didn't matter. The guards were gone.

* * * * * * *

The girls ran up to the gates, but there was no sign of Finn. Then, just as a sick feeling of panic washed over Yaz, she heard a sound like a strangled elephant. It was the noise the van's engine made when Finn was driving it at full throttle!

The van smashed through the gates. Finn spun it round to face back the way he'd come.

'OK, all on board,' shouted Yaz.

The girls high-fived each other then scrambled inside and the van roared off into the night.

An MIB officer wearing a huge pair of ear defenders came running up to the gates and watched them go.

'You have won this time,' he muttered. 'But we will track you down. You can run, but there is nowhere you can hide from us.'

Will the Zargons ever defeat *GirlFriendZ* ?

What do you think?